The Sea Egg

The Sea Egg

L. M. BOSTON

illustrated by

PETER BOSTON

FABER AND FABER LTD
London

First published in 1967
by Faber and Faber Limited
24 Russell Square London WC1
First published in this edition 1970
Printed in Great Britain by
Latimer Trend & Co Ltd Plymouth
All rights reserved

SBN (paper edition) 571 09389 2
SBN (cloth edition) 571 08111 8

FOR
CAROLINE

The tide was going out when Toby and Jo looked out of the window in the early morning. There were no waves, but the sea was smooth and blue like a looking-glass reflecting the sky, and was slowly sinking back from the beach with hardly a ripple.

It was a magical morning with a silence like all the secrets in the world, and a light like happiness. As the boys ran down the slope towards the sea the stones skidded and clattered under their feet, making a great noise in the quiet morning. The gulls were all peacefully riding the sleepy sea and nobody else was about, except a man bringing in his boat with the lobsters he had caught in his pots by the headland.

The boys knew him. He had a shack at the side of the cliff path where he cut and polished stones to make souvenirs for visitors, and sometimes he took people out in his boat. He now came up the beach, carrying a basket full of lobsters on his head. They rattled against each other and clawed on the basketwork with their awkward limbs, and their stiff feelers waved above the rim.

"'Morning," said the man ."It'll be a scorcher later on. But when I set out at five o'clock it was the loveliest morning you could wish to see. The sort of day when, if

9

you were by yourself, you could imagine—well, anything you liked."

"Mermaids?" said Toby.

"Never seen one of them yet. But I fetched up something in my lobster pot that I've never seen before either."

He put his hand in his pocket and pulled out a stone which he handed to Jo. It was warm from his pocket and was the size of a turkey's egg. It was green, veined with white and speckled with black.

"See that? It's egg-shaped. You can search on the beach all your days and find all sorts of shapes, but never a regular egg-shape. The sea just doesn't make them."

Jo cupped it in his hands and shifted it caressingly from one to the other. He loved it and wanted it.

"It's a Sea Egg," he said.

"There's no such a thing," said the man, holding out his hand to take it back.

"Let me see it too." Toby and Jo handled it between them as if their four hands belonged to the same person. They were both certain that the sea egg was what they wanted most in the world.

The man still held out his hand. "I'm going to polish it," he said. "Somebody will buy it, if I have to wait till next Easter."

The two boys followed it with their eyes till it disappeared into the man's pocket.

He began to move away up the beach, leaving them standing in silence. When he was half-way up and going more slowly because the stones were bigger and more uneven, the two boys ran after him and Toby, all out of breath, managed to overtake him and stand in his way.

"How much will it be?" he asked, while Jo stumbled and clambered to get there in time.

The man looked at their excitement with surprise.

"How much will what be?"

"The sea egg, when it's polished."

"Oh, that! I'd forgotten all about it."

"But how much will it be?"

"That depends on who wants it, and how badly. If it's a rich American with no sense it might be a pound or two. If it's a local grandmother who wants to darn her old man's socks on it, I might give it her for nothing."

"What if it was boys?"

"What would boys want it for? Breaking windows? I wouldn't sell it to boys."

"What," said Jo desperately, "if a boy's father wanted to buy it? How much would it be then?"

"I'd charge at least five bob for polishing it. Now let me get on. I've got to deliver these lobsters at the hotel." He moved on.

The boys sat down on the stones to take counsel. Their way of doing this was simply to sit in silence thinking about the same thing. They sat side by side hugging their knees till suddenly Toby said, "Let's look. He might be teasing us." They ran down to the lower part of the cove where the smallest stones were heaped up in a bank, and began to search among them. There were flat ovals by the million and flat pear-shapes, occasional perfect ping-pong or billiard balls, sausages, nuts, and beautiful irregular shapes that have no name. There were plenty of eggs, if only eggs were not bigger at one end than the other, or if they were flat instead of round. But that is what an egg is—rounded, and bigger at one end than the other. And as the man had said, that didn't seem to happen.

At last they stood up and looked around, and there was the sea, huge and wide and blue, and so full of light it seemed hardly to be there at all, but it heaved gently as if it breathed in its sleep, and whispered in an echoey way, both near and very far off.

"Well then," said Toby, "come on." He was running up the shore and Jo after him.

"I don't wonder you got up so early," said their mother as she filled their plates. "What a day!"

"Afraid I slept," said their father from behind a newspaper. "The sea was so quiet."

"It was out," said Jo with his mouth full.

"What were you doing?"

"Watching the lobster man." Toby's eyes met Jo's for an instant, but there was no need to exchange signs.

"Did he have a good catch?"

"Umm," Jo nodded with his mouth full again.

"All right. Get on with your breakfast. We've nearly finished ours."

"Umm."

Jo put down his spoon before Toby. He wiped his mouth with deliberation as if leaving nothing undone before going into careful action. He went casually to his mother and leant against her till she put her arm round him to show that she had noticed.

"Mum?"

"What, darling?"

"Mum, can I have some money?"

"What do you want it for this time?"

He pulled at her shoulder so that she leant to him, but his half whisper could be clearly heard.

"I want to get Toby a present."

"Do you, darling? Can I know what it is?"

"It's a secret. It's something he wants quite terribly badly."

"Does it cost a lot?"

"Could you spare half a crown?"

"Yes, I think so. I hope it isn't for ice-cream."

Jo shook his head. The half-crown was handed over with a show of secrecy.

Toby then laid down his spoon and went to his father.

"Can I have half a crown too?" he asked openly. "Mum's given some to Jo." Then he whispered in his ear so that nobody could possibly hear, though of course they did. "It's for Jo really."

A second half-crown was fetched up out of the trouser pocket and the parents looked at each other with eyes that clearly said, "What nice boys we have got."

This successfully done, the boys whooped and ran out.

When they reached the shack the shutters had been taken down ready for the day's trade, but the door was closed. The boys were so impatient they couldn't believe it. They knocked and rattled, but the padlock was there clearly to be seen, and it was fastened.

"I thought he'd have finished his breakfast by now."

"We'll have to wait."

They looked idly in the window at all the things made out of stones from the beach, the lighthouses of all sizes, the vases and fascinating lidded boxes, the brooches, the ash-trays and ash-trays and ash-trays.

"Oh look! there it is. There, on his bench."

They had to bend sideways to see it because of a shelf across the window full of objects for sale, and then they were lucky if they could see it with one eye behind the reflections of themselves and the view on the glass.

"He's polished it already!"

The inside of the shack was rather dark, but over the walls the shimmer of the sea threw rippled lights and shadows, and these played with an extra liveliness over the polished egg where it lay beside a heap of uncut stones.

"It looks as if it were still in the sea."

"In a rock pool, because it looks wet and the big pieces round it look dry."

"That's because it's been polished. I wonder if it matters being polished?"

"Do you think it could?"

"Well, if you were a sea egg, being whizzed scorching hot on a lathe would feel funny. And it would make the shell thinner."

"I want to put it in a rock pool."

"I wish he would come."

They continued to gaze with their faces against the

14

glass, their elbows spread and their sandal toes scuffing the gravel.

"Toby!!" Jo's voice was electric.

"What?"

"I think it's moving. Sort of rocking."

"What do you mean, rocking? Oh, I see. It could be the ripple shadows wiggling over it, couldn't it?"

But the egg did seem now and again to rock with a little movement like impatience.

"O dear! I wish he would come. He must eat a huge breakfast."

A hard but friendly hand walloped the seat of Toby's shorts.

"So I do. I need it. *And* I polished your egg before I had any. I thought you'd be back for it. I suppose that's what you've come for?"

"Yes."

"And I don't mind admitting I was a bit fascinated by it myself. Can't place what kind of stone it is. Never seen this marking before."

He stood looking at it as if he had all day for contemplation. Jo and Toby could hardly breathe for fear that tell-tale wobble should happen again and the man say, "Hi! what's this? I can't let you have that."

It seemed a very long time that they all stood there in silence. Then Toby took charge. He held out his hand for Jo's half-crown and then offered them both on his palm to the man.

"Thank you for polishing it," he said. "We will take it now."

The lobster man handed it over as though suddenly losing interest. "Want it wrapped up?" He pulled out a rather dirty piece of newspaper.

"No!!" said Jo, and having prevented what he felt was an outrage to the Sea Egg, he added a belated, "Thank you all the same."

Toby cupped the shining thing in his hands and the two boys walked off in a brisk practical way as if they had been buying some simple thing such as grit for a canary.

As soon as they were out of sight of the shack the boys sat down on a rock and considered the egg as it lay in a cradle made of their four hands. Below them the sea whispered restlessly as if it had lost something and would soon come in, moving further and further toward the cliffs, turning the sand over this way and that as it came, and heaping up its indignant depth until it found what had been taken from it.

The boys heard this sea talk with more than the usual shiver of awe when the tide turns.

Toby suddenly drew his fingers away from under the egg.

"It's hatching," he said, "I felt it tap."

A second later Jo spilled it off hastily on to the sand.

"What if it's a sea-serpent?"

"It will only be a baby one. We could tame it."

"Its mother might come and eat us."

"Perhaps it's a sea ogre. Ogres keep their souls in eggs."

The boys made their worst possible ogre faces at each other, with ghost noises to match. Then they sobered down and turned to watch the egg again.

"Perhaps it's a storm egg and will hatch out a terrible great storm."

"A great white sea horse that will claw down cliffs."

"A sea genie that will do whatever we ask."

"I hope it isn't just a sea-cow."

"Would cows come out of eggs?"

"Fishes do. I don't know how fishy a sea-cow is. But it's very ugly in the sea book."

"This is a very beautiful egg," said Jo. "I would like a sea-horse."

"We've got to know what it is, anyway. We must find a secret place for it, so that nobody catches it to stuff it for the Museum."

"Somewhere where it can't easily get out. Because we can't stay there all the time. I suppose it has to be in the water."

"I know. Our rock pool."

"Come on then."

The rock pool which the boys felt was their own was in the most distant part of the coastline that they had reached in their scrambles along the base of the cliffs. It was in the next cove, which could only be entered through a natural tunnel in the headland, and that only at low tide. For two or three hours when the tide was out, the tunnel and the desert island cove beyond it were perfectly safe, and for the first person to enter it the cove showed newly washed sand and boulders, hung with newly rinsed and combed seaweed hair, studded with glossy sea anemones newly closed up, and never a footprint in sight. At such a moment it was startlingly sea-private and no one entered it without a feeling of daring. As the tide rose, and long before it was at the full, the tunnel was submerged, at first only by the farthest push of a frothy ripple, then by a stronger swirl, deepening ever more quickly till it became the meeting place for savage waves approaching from both sides of the headland and slapping up in an angry explosion in the middle.

The boys knew that the tide had turned to come in, but they knew too that it never broke its rules or came too soon, unless driven by a howling gale or tossed up by an earthquake. This was a perfect day and they had time enough for their purpose, yet as their bare feet pressed the ribbed sand that floored the tunnel and the warm sun was cut off from their backs, as their hands felt the eternal cold of the water-polished sides and they looked up at the downward pointing rocks of the roof, they remembered with shivers how the sea goes about its business.

The tunnel was not long, but it had a bend in the middle and a central pillar helping to hold up the chaotic tumble of jammed rocks that made its roof. There was no arch or keystone here to give confidence that the sea would not some day tear it down.

They were glad to come out on to the bright sand of the inner cove. Full as it was of unimaginable sea wonders they did not stop to savour even the things they loved most. The soft ticking in the wet sand as bubbles burst in it was like a sea clock, ticking away the allowed minutes.

Toby and Jo pattered straight across the cove to the

outlying rocks on the far side, where once the face of the cliff had fallen down.

Here there was much scrambling to be done, at which they were as agile as a pair of dogs—up and down, this way and that, sometimes finding they could go no further, confronted by a slab higher than their fingers could reach, so that they had to retrace their steps, slithering down with difficulty where it had been easy to go up; over smooth humps where they wriggled spread-eagled, between ravines, through cracks, passing every moment rock pools of great charm and variety, till they reached their own special pool.

It was well walled in with smooth blocks of rock and the curves of immense boulders that lay half buried. Or perhaps it was only their bald heads sticking out, and like icebergs that are seven times bigger than you can see, they went down under a great way.

To enter the pool you went out of a small enclosure like a porch, up stone steps, through a narrow vertical opening, and down further steps into a magical bath. It was so well built it was hard to believe that it was accidental, and yet had it been made on purpose it could never have taken your breath away with delight as it did.

The clear, warm, still water in it had a rich sea-scape of pools within pools, on shelves or in rock pockets, with pink sea-lace fringes and pebbles shining like beads on the bottom of a jewel box. It had smooth crimson stones as seats where you could sit up to your armpits in water. At one end was a narrow crack, well protected from the force of the waves by an immovable barrier of rocks outside, through which, when the tide rose, lovely gushes and playful cascades of sea water came in, till it was deep enough for a boy to swim in, to turn and glide and float, and if he had a snorkel to see his shadow on the pebbles beneath him.

Toby and Jo slid with serious joy into its shallow water, as blue as the sky till their paddling broke it up.

Surely no better place than this could be found for a rare sea-creature, whatever it should turn out to be. It would hardly need at first to move out into a larger space, and while still weak from hatching would not be battered by rough waves. Best of all, for more than half of every day it would be quite cut off, which greatly increased its chance of not being seen.

The boys placed the egg in the middle of the pool, in the deepest part, and after hovering round it lovingly for a time they climbed out to lie sprawled over the rocks to watch it. They waited till the disturbed water had settled again to perfect stillness, then waited on in the hope that the glassy surface would shake a little and betray a wobble from the egg beneath it.

The sun was hot on their backs. They were hemmed in by silent bare rocks which cut them off from sight of either the cove or the tunnel. It was a landscape like the beginning of the world, with magic enough and suddenly no comfort. Anything might happen. The thought of prehistoric monsters was real, and there were nameless thoughts of things that perhaps never had happened, but might, in this hot silence that seemed to be before noise had been born.

Jo sidled nearer to Toby and looked round anxiously, above and below. Toby was still watching the pool when its water was shaken and clouded and the lower fringes of seaweed gently stirred. It was the first touch of the creeping waveless tide.

Jo was anxious to start for home at once, but Toby waited obstinately, more disappointed than frightened, though he was that too. When the pool was half filled with restless tide water and the boulders leading to it were becoming islands one after the other, with pockets of deep water between them where you could step down up to your thigh when you least expected it, the boys began the return scramble, leaving their precious five shillings' worth in its sea cradle. The sea had taken it.

When they arrived in sight of the cove and on the far side of it the headland where the tunnel was, there was a reassuring stretch of dry sand that showed time enough and to spare. Nevertheless they ran, in swoops and swerves as boys do, and reached the tunnel while it was still dry. It showed only two sets of footprints, their own Coming through it on to the more public beach they found that too still almost empty. People were only now beginning to climb down the cliff path with their picnic baskets. It startled the boys to find inside themselves such a feeling of endless time already experienced before the day had properly started.

They skirmished about near the mouth of the tunnel as if on guard, sitting on rocks till the tide cut them off, then splashing their way out. It was so hot that land clothes or bathing clothes made no difference. What did it matter that they were in shirts and shorts?

They had never yet seen this usually boisterous sea so silky and waveless and inexorably rising. It was harder to gauge its depth, and there were no sudden sucked withdrawals of the water through which one could dash between wave and wave. When it began to cover the floor of the tunnel the boys went back through it again, to emphasize how much time there was still in hand. They waited as long as their nerves would allow, and returned through a cave water-patterned over walls and roof, and to their senses coming alive. Like the dry sandy seaweed and the limpets, it was part of the sea and welcomed it back.

With water up to their knees they did it again. This was easy—no rough waves were coming through to slap them in the mouth, and one must learn what one dare do. There was no dry land on the far side now, and the heave of the sea was stronger. They returned through water up to their waists, feeling the roof of the tunnel too close over their heads, and whichever way they looked out they saw nothing but sea.

"No one else will go through today," said Toby as they pushed and splashed through the water that lay between the mouth of the tunnel and the dry home beach.

Their mother was standing at the edge of the water, looking anxiously inland beyond the cottage. Oddly enough they were surprised to see her. In those last chilling moments in the tunnel they had forgotten her existence! Now she saw them and waved and looked very happy, and they ran through the wide shallows, kicking out their feet sideways and making an arch of spray over themselves till they arrived beside her, their shirts and shorts plastered to their bodies.

"You wretches!" she laughed, "coming back like dogs that have had a private swim! Where have you been? I was beginning to be worried. And I should have been more worried if I had known you were on the other side of the tunnel. You left it late to come through. You *know* you could get cut off."

"Of course we know, Mum. And we didn't leave it till the last minute. We've been here ages, but we kept going through again as long as we could."

"For practice," said Jo. "And there are no waves."

"I thought you'd gone to the village shopping."

Jo thought of the shop and its contents.

"Can I have a bun?" he said.

"Me too."

As the tide was now covering the beach and would soon cover it completely, the family went up along the cliffs for their picnic. Their father took field-glasses as he always did. There was much to watch—birds, ships, helicopters. Today the special object of the excursion was seals, because of the unusual clearness of the water.

It was hot walking up the slopes in blazing sun, and when their mother said, "Let's sit down here a moment. I'm so hot, and there's nothing more I can take off," they were high up above their pool.

They sat near the edge of the precipice that had been

left when long ago that barrier of rock had fallen out-ward and crashed into the sea. The field-glasses were handed to everyone in turn.

Down there below, the pale delicious water was so clear that all the bottom could be seen. The only differ-ence between rocks above water and rocks below was a subtle change in colour. In patches the seaweed could be seen growing upright like plants, spreading branches.

Even without the glasses the boys could see their pool, its walls deep beneath the liquid living blue. They searched it with the glasses, but could not identify their egg on the bottom. Yes, no, yes, no, they said in turn. How far down under the tide would it be? Ten feet? Fifteen feet? A seagull was resting on the water just above the pool. It looked near enough for them to dive in be-side it. They could see its pink feet idly paddling. The sun bit into their bent backs.

"Here comes the helicopter," said their father. "Hand me the glasses a moment."

From gazing down into coolness they turned to gaze up into the burning sky.

Later in the day, past the next headland but one, they did see seals, two of them. Toby, who had a proper re-spect for waves, had imagined seals living a desperate life always, awake or asleep, ready to avoid the crash of a ton of water. These two, the first he had seen, appeared the idlest creatures imaginable, not needing or caring to make a movement of any kind. They floated, not horizontally as we do, but upright like half-sunk bottles, their noses sticking out. Now and again with a lazy half turn they sank under water and could be seen moving like slow balloons among the rocks, to come up somewhere else, as if for a change of view.

"They are having the kind of holiday Daddy likes," said Jo. (Their father was at this moment asleep on his back, pillowed in heather.) Well, perhaps that was it. Perhaps they could, in a storm, flash like lithe leaping salmon. Their faces, seen through the glasses, were human, but not in the unflattering way that monkeys' are. (For one thing they had no visible ears.) They had domed heads and huge gentle eyes, and the same vague expression that all humans have when floating for pleasure. The sea is the whole of their thought.

That night as Toby and Jo lay side by side in the big double bed which is what seaside lodgings usually provide, their last thoughts were of their pool, now emptying again, reflecting the young moon. They had wanted to go there again before bedtime, but it was dark before they could have reached the tunnel, and their hearts failed them. They comforted themselves that their parents would certainly have said No. We'll go first thing tomorrow, they promised each other.

"I expect it was only a stone really," said Jo. But when he fell asleep he dreamt that he was trying to climb the cliff to escape from an octopus, but it saw him with its horrible eyes like field-glasses, and came after him. As it had eight limbs to climb with to his four, he had no hope of escaping, and it was when the fishy tentacle caught him round the waist that his mother, but not Toby, was wakened by his cries.

The next morning was even better. The tide, as every young Briton should know in his bones, is fifty minutes later every day. When at breakfast the boys said they wanted to go beyond the tunnel, their parents said, "Yes, let's all go together." The boys had kept their secret, not because they wanted their parents kept out, but just because to keep an idea secret is almost to make it true. After his last night's nightmare Jo was relieved to have the grown-ups with him.

"I expect it was only a stone really," he repeated to Toby as they left their parents comfortably lying in the sun in the inner cove, and went on themselves towards their pool.

"It was a Sea Egg," said Toby firmly. They approached warily, creeping round the rocks with exaggerated care. The water of the pool was as flat and still as a window-pane. Nothing plopped or flipped, nothing was heard moving on the rocks, no dislodgement of pebbles, no dry scaly rustle, no squawk of startled newly hatched roc or pterodactyl. At last they ventured into the pool itself, putting each foot down with precaution so as not to cloud the water and perhaps disturb something they had not seen. They searched the pool from end to end, and finally scuffed up the bottom with their toes to feel if there was anything lying covered by the veins of drifting sand.

"Such as a bit of egg shell," said Jo. He did pick up a piece of fractured curved stone, but except that the edges were sharp there was nothing about it. He threw it back, then later found another piece and would have liked to try if the edges matched. But the first piece could not be found again.

The boys leant against the side of the "bath" and felt there was nothing left for them to do or play or think. The tide, not quite so waveless as yesterday, swished its first little burst of water into the pool where Toby was standing, and they heard their father calling for them.

"I did rather think," said Toby as they turned to go, "that I heard a kind of tail swish in that covered crack where the sea comes in. But it could have been just the water gurgling. Only, it did sound like something that had been hiding there and was glad the tide was coming back. The tide makes it more private for anything."

"Did you really?" asked Jo, who was feeling rather common-sensical. But Toby could not say he was sure.

Jo marched up to his mother.

"Somebody's taken our stone Sea Egg," he said. "We were making an aquarium and we put it in. It was beautiful. And now there is nothing."

"I don't suppose anybody took it," said their mother. "Most probably the sand covered it up. Turtles lay their eggs on the edge of the sea specially to make sure it happens."

"If a turtle was hiding under the sand," said Toby, taking up the idea, "you could tread on its back and not know it wasn't a stone."

"Is a turtle a tortoise big enough to ride on? We could ride it down the beach."

"It would be very lurchy over the rocks," said their

mother, always ready to join in. "Worse than an elephant. Its legs are too short. Always clawing in empty space and then trusting to luck as it skids down. Think of a tortoise on a rockery."

"We had all sorts of ideas," said Toby sadly.

"Well, ideas are free," said their father briskly. "You'll have to get some more. How about going out in a motor boat while it's so calm? We can go along the coast, have lunch in a different cove, and get back about six. Look."

He spread his map on a boulder and showed them the buoys and the lighthouse and the islands, the races, and the beaches where no one could ever set foot except from a boat at certain times in calm weather, and the rocks where ships were most often wrecked and where the last could still be seen, a rusty old iron hulk broken-backed and crumpled on the cliff foot.

They gathered up their things and set off homeward, and the tunnel when they walked through it was just an ordinary safe-as-houses passage, the sea still far away.

The lobster man took them in his little boat. He preferred to come with them.

"This is no coastline for strangers to play about in, however experienced. You've got to be brought up on it. It has its own ways and moods and you must know the tricks. The sea's your master here. You want to tickle it and humour it to get by. But some visitors think they can ignore the race with a 2 h.p. engine."

"Then do they get drowned?" asked Jo, hopeful of dramatic justice and fearful of possible personal adventures.

"Not often," the man answered casually. "But there's rescue parties have to go out. And that usually means me. Or they may find themselves glad to get in somewhere where they never meant to go."

When the engine first started up, the noise, re-echoing to them from the circling cliffs of the cove, seemed very loud and they had to shout to be heard. Soon everybody gave up speaking, and the fascination of seeing the familiar formation of the shore taking its place at a distance as a stage scene on which they had no part to play would have kept them silent anyway.

Once past the headland everything was strange. They were in the open sea, much less smooth than it looked, and in fact they positively met it with a bump. The land was now only a wall of cliffs, stretching on either side as far as they could see and seeming nearly to close in a circle round them. But the space of water contained in this shimmering space was so vast that the sound of their motor seemed to die out, losing its busy importance in the immensity.

They passed round an island close off shore, whose landward side they knew well, but they had not imagined what a ravaged face it presented to seaward. The sea had been savagely working at it for thousands of years and had mined three deep caves in it, and there was another opening high up on the cliff face. These opened behind the ruins of earlier caves, of which nothing was left but two arches rising out of the water, the very land under which the arches went having been washed away.

They were rounding the island through surprisingly choppy water, keeping well out, as even on this windless day the water round its seaward foot was torn into white fluttering ribbons by the sunken rocks. When the tide was running out strongly, the lobster man told them, this would be the race, and in a storm the island got the full force of wind and waves.

Jo wanted to know if seals sheltered in caves when there was a storm.

"Not in cliff-face caves," said the man. "That would be the worst place they could choose. The waves would pound them to pulp. But these caves are said to lead by an underwater passage to a place under the island where there's a pool that's always calm. A good place to shelter if you knew a storm was brewing and got there before the waves were too rough in the entrance."

"Do you mean the island's hollow?"

"That's right."

The boys shot excited questions at him in turn.

"Would seals know that a storm was coming?"

"I guess they would. If they didn't know the ways of the sea they wouldn't last long."

"Have you ever been in that hollow place?"

"I've been in the cave mouth, but I don't swim, let alone under water."

"Do you mean you don't know how to swim?"

"If you're in a boat you don't need to."

"What if your boat was wrecked?"

The man laughed. "I'm like the seals, I've got the know-how, them in the water and me in the dry."

"Daddy, I'd like to go into that seal place. Couldn't we some time with my snorkel?"

Toby felt he was almost dying with desire. But at the thought of a dark rock-hall cut off from the world by a tunnel underwater, Jo felt as much terror as excitement, though what Toby did he would do.

"Your snorkel would be no good in an underwater passage. There would be no air for it to bring you."

Their father was examining the caves through his field-glasses. He handed them to Toby. "See if you can see any seals there. I can't. And we don't know how long the tunnel is. Seals can go a long way without breathing. Anyway we'd need a seal to guide us. The island may be a labyrinth inside."

The boys looked at the island with wonder. It had seemed from the shore weighty and solid and everlasting. Now it was known to be a structure of buckling and toppling pillars, of undermined foundations and echoing cavities, with just a covering of gravel and grass over the top that would vanish easily some day under the sweep of the sea.

"How long has the island been there?"

Toby was anxious to know if the cliffs they walked on every day would last out the holidays. His father's answer was reassuring up to a point.

"They say there was a Bronze Age settlement on it. The island must have been considerably bigger 4,000 years ago, as well as being joined on to the mainland.

You can see a row of rock islands where it used to join up. I imagine the smaller it gets the quicker it goes."

"Like toffee," said Jo.

They had now passed the island and were crossing the cove where the boys' pool lay.

Toby still had the field-glasses. Suddenly he called out, "There are seals! There are seals on the big flat rock by our pool!"

Jo looked and his voice broke into a high squeak. "There are two baby seals!"

Everybody looked in turn, but the boys' excitement was so great that in the end the glasses were left to them, and shared between them with remarkable fairness. The lobster man shut off speed while they looked.

Toby focused carefully. The mother seal lay on the big rock. She was sleek and shining from the sea, a noble-looking animal, her throat elegantly speckled, like a thrush. Two silver-grey pups lay at the edge of the brimming pool near her. They had the round unexpectant faces of well-fed babies, their noses pink, their heavy-lidded eyes just closing. All three seemed preparing for a snooze in the sun, while the sea breathed and sighed all round them. They appeared to be close to the end of the field-glasses, like a secret vision that disappeared when the boat rocked.

"I think there must be a third young one, just behind the mother." Toby handed the glasses to Jo.

Jo also found the fairy-tale picture, held as it were at the end of his nose. Something did seem to be behind the mother seal's shoulder, because she looked round at it in a motherly sort of way.

Toby had the glasses again and there was a tense silence. The seal had reared up and with her flippers pushed a radiant little creature in front of her. It was smaller than her pups but very active.

"*It's got a boy's face!*"

The grown-ups in the boat looked on indulgently at the boys who were trembling with excitement.

"Very human-looking things, seals," said the lobster man. "I could never kill one."

The boys had gone as quiet as if they were in a shared trance. Jo had snatched the glasses to see this creature with a boy's face, and there it was, with its blond head and its big black eyes like the seals', and a small boy's impish smile. It was Toby who saw it stroke the seal's neck, and Jo in his turn who saw the double tail, rose- and

34

emerald-scaled, merrily flipping in the air as a child lying on its back waves its legs. The seal gave it a gentle nudge with her nose. It rolled over, crawling on its fishy knees, and plopped obediently into the pool.

If two faces could have shared one pair of glasses the boys would have done so. They had seen, whatever the lobster man said, a sea-boy. Baby seals don't have two coral and green tails, or hands. Speechless, they let the glasses be taken from their double grasp.

"I only saw two babies," said their father. "They've all taken to the water now. Well, you were lucky. You had a good look at them. I think we had better put on speed now, we have a fair way to go."

The boat revved up and ploughed along through the sea, while the boys sat shoulder to shoulder and gazed backward towards the cove in case anything should surface again, until they were round the next headland and out of sight. Then they just sat and thought.

"You two are very silent," said their mother. "You can't be feeling sick, can you?"

" 'Course not," said Jo angrily. "But I'm hot, the seat's hot, the sides of the boat are hot."

The lobster man said there were clouds coming up on the south that meant thunder by night-time. "We'll turn in at Drift Cove. You've time for a picnic there, and then it would be wise to get back."

Every cove is individual like a new country, very different from the next one to it, even when they share a headland. Nearly always there is a little stream coming from inland that has eaten its way through the softest soil and convenient cracks in the rock till it reaches the beach, or, if it is still too young to have carved itself a channel, oozes in a slow dribble over the cliffs.

Drift Cove, where the lobster man now drew in, had a lively brook down the centre, which talked to itself as it wriggled and twisted its way between the packed stones of the upper shore but was silent to all but the keenest ear when it reached the sand. Its course across the sand opened out like a large fan, and the water, though hardly deep enough to float a match-box, had yet moulded the sand that it flowed over into a regular all-over pattern of small fans. Through this the family waded, spoiling its precisely decorated bed, to reach a comfortably curved grass bank that they saw higher up.

The boat was left moored to an iron ring in the rock by a tiny natural landing place. The boatman went striding off up the cliff path to a friend's cottage out of sight.

Drift Cove was famous for its shells. Its bright pinky-white sand was made entirely of shell dust, like star-dust, among which, if you sifted it through your fingers, were infant shells as small as the grains but perfectly shaped. Scattered over the surface were larger shells of many kinds and shapes, some as delicate as flower petals, others, though small, built to withstand any battering sea. The boys collected beauties to put in their pool. They had their own reason for wishing to do this, and continued thoughtful and silent.

On the way to the chosen picnic place they passed three large baskets with money-boxes confidingly tied to them, bearing a notice DEEP SEA SHELLS 2s. each. Whoever was in charge had evidently gone home to lunch.

The first basket was full of sea-urchin shells, as big as cricket balls, but as light as air and as brittle as eggshell. They were shaped like luscious ripe fruits, all of different pink and plum colours, with patterns of raised beads like seed pearls. Each one was an object rich and rare enough to have been brought as his gift by one of the Three Kings of Orient.

The second basket contained large heavy shells of widely different shapes, some like wide-mouthed deep sea lilies, some almost as fantastic as spaniels' ears carved in white jade by a Chinese artist, but all with a rich glaze over their colour and all magically inhabited by profound sea-murmurs.

The third basket was full of necklaces of curled shells threaded together, speckled cowries or striped water snails.

Their mother, wondering if the boys were still grieving for the loss of their stone egg—you never know why children get a passion for one special thing—told them they could choose one each for their aquarium. She put the money in the boxes.

Jo could not resist the sea urchins, but Toby, after turning all the big shells over and trying each one to his own and everyone's ear, ended by choosing a tapering spiral shell about eight inches long. It was not that it held the best sound of West Indian waves, but because its sound was singular and unmistakable, more like a voice than the sea, and seemed addressed to him personally. He let Jo listen to it.

"It's a secret," he told him.

While they were eating their sandwiches Toby, as the eldest, approached the question that was swamping all other thought.

"Daddy, do you believe in mermaids?"

"I should hate not to," he answered and pulling a half-funny face.

"But do you?" insisted Jo. "Are they real?"

"Ask your mother."

"You are mean," she said.

"Mummy, do you believe in mermaids?"

"I know I shouldn't, but I can never quite help it."

"Well done," said their father.

"Well then, Mummy, if there are mermaids wouldn't there have to be mermen?"

"Tritons they are called." Their father rolled lazily over on to his other elbow. "They blow wreathéd horns. Like the shell Toby bought in fact."

"What do they blow horns for?"

"To signal to their friends; to call up their sea-horses; to announce a moonlight frolic; to warn of approaching storms. What would you use a trumpet for?"

Toby looked at his shell. "It has a hole in the top. You could blow it."

His father held out a hand. "Shall I try?"

"No," said Toby clutching his shell. "I don't want you to. It's special."

"You are right. It is special. It's a left-handed one. That's a good 2s.'s worth. The fisherman can't have known. Collectors will give a lot of money for left-handed ones."

"Why are they better, Daddy?"

"For one thing, they are rare. And they are supposed to be magic. Perhaps it's a good thing I didn't blow it before I noticed."

Jo was holding his sea urchin up to the sky and looking through the hole in the bottom.

"It won't float," he said. "I thought it would be a sea-ball, but it has tiny needle holes all over it. It would sink. I am going to change it."

He went back to the baskets and returned with a necklace of cowrie shells, weighing it lovingly between his hands.

"Is that a present for your mother?"

"No," he answered in embarrassment. "It's for cutting teeth on."

The parents laughed, because Jo was losing his first teeth, and Toby laughed, because he knew they were laughing at the wrong thing. And Jo laughed most, because he enjoyed the feeling.

The clouds meanwhile were piling steadily up in the south, leaning over the top of the sky. At the same time a thick haze was forming underneath them and spreading over the sea, which changed in colour under it from blue to purple and from purple to slate. The heat seemed greater without the sun, as if an incubator had been spread over the world.

They saw the lobster man signalling to them from the boat.

When they came to cross the stream again, it had perfectly remade its beautiful creased patterns while they were having lunch, and was as new as if intruders had

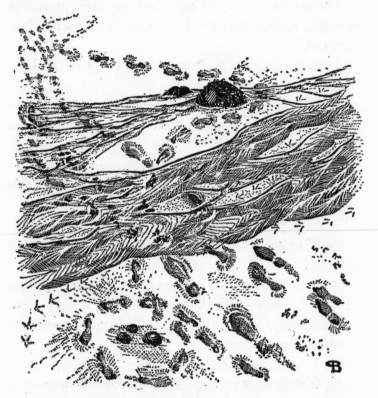

never existed. They had to undo its work again, but the moment they had crossed over it began industriously to recreate its soft sand fans which seemed to have a part to play in the order of the universe.

The boat roared straight out to sea, over fidgety

water. The surface of the slow heaves was no longer smooth, but faceted like badly cut jewellery, little angular planes tipped in every direction and jostling without seeming to have momentum. It fretted and nibbled at the sides of the boat.

They passed the triton's cove too far out to see anything, even if the heat haze had not been wrapping them in. Beyond the island the boatman turned them into the race, which he said was not running out strongly yet as the tide had only just turned. Nevertheless there were steely undulations running east, across which the boat, travelling with the current and twice as fast as before, bounded and bucked with an action like a slow gallop with jumps, and the bows plunged with a hard thud into the next rise. The boys, who were inexperienced sailors, gripped the boat and had little thought to spare for caves.

"We'll soon be out of this," the lobster man assured their mother. "It's nothing to what we'd have got if we had waited. There's a backwater further on that will get us out. There'll be a thunder storm all right later. You can feel the sea's uneasy."

"The seals will know," said Jo, rather white in the face.

The boat walloped along past Home Cove, while the boatman edged it in, then suddenly turned in a wide arc full-throttle toward the shore and they were in the backwater and the slap bang sea-saw motion was changed to a comfortable jog.

They came in at last to Home Cove, past their tunnel half filled with the ebbing tide, and the boat was run on to the shelving sand. The boys jumped out, not succeeding in missing the swirl of sea-lace that each wave spread round them. They were feeling a little sick and heartily thankful to be out of the boat.

The lobster man proved right. When the tide was at dead ebb under breathless cloud the lightning began.

Toby and Jo got out of bed to watch. It was sheet lightning that flickered round the horizon, with occasional brilliant blue filaments that jigged up and down, vividly lighting the surly sea and the sharp outline of the island. Thunder was growling here, there, and everywhere, apparently without reference to the lightning and seldom with any definite detonation. Finally the imprisoned cloud broke, hurling down rain in such density that, in the last of the flashes, the boys saw nothing through their window but an electric blaze of flying raindrops.

All that night it rained, and in the morning Toby and Jo looked out at a world huddled under a steady downpour. The sea was rumpled and grumbling. It threw its ebbing, ineffectual waves at the shore like someone leaving in a petty temper. From the distance of their cottage its noise was half drowned in the patter and gurgle of rain. In the intermittent gusts of wind the rain too dashed its thin waves on window-panes and puddles.

The grown-ups sighed and looked out and sighed again. They made plans for going by car somewhere, perhaps to see an aircraft carrier that had come into port thirty miles away. They were surprised at the boys' lack of interest.

Toby and Jo were of course burning to go to their pool. After all, you can't quite believe in the appearing and disappearing pictures you see in field-glasses. But they had great hopes.

"We want to put our shells in the pool first," they said imploringly. "It doesn't matter that it is raining. We don't mind."

"Let them go," said their father. "The tide is down and quite safe, and there are two of them. If one slips and breaks a leg the other can come back and tell us. Use your sense, boys, and don't try to climb the cliffs."

They put on their black oilskins and sou'westers, but refused gumboots. "Not for the *shore*," said Jo indignantly.

The shore was utterly deserted. At first sight half its charm was gone when there was no division between the wet sea and the dry land, but all was equally grey and wet. It was however wilder, and different, with all the stones enamelled instead of only those touched by the sea, and all the seaweed plump and smelling of iodine. The rain made an orchestra of different sounds, falling on stone, or sand, or muting seaweed, or water, as well as gurgling and dripping. It was loudest on their oilskins. It pestered the boys, driving in their faces. Toby had long eyelashes which were plastered together. If he raised a hand to wipe his face, the water ran down his sleeve. Their oilskins rattled as they walked and the sou'westers made it difficult to hear.

In the tunnel at least they were dry and could open their eyes. They were surprised to see how the rain-soaked land above it drained in oozes through the roof, reminding them now that they had seen the far side of the island, how water seeps in, licks away and prises open, ready for the sea to dynamite and sweep away.

Toby and Jo walked across the heavy sand not saying much, but the awareness of what they hoped to see made the veiled landscape more mysterious and above all, wonderfully secret. It was a private day for the sea, when it might carelessly show some aspect of itself that was usually hidden. Torn curtains of rain blew into the mouths of far coves, hiding the further headlands, and the fish-grey waves when they broke sounded heavier for being cold.

When the boys reached the rocks they sheltered under an overhang, needing to talk.

"Go very carefully," Toby said. "Remember we only saw him through field-glasses. He hasn't seen us. He might be frightened."

"He might think," said Jo, finding it was harder to scramble on rocks in a heavy oilskin, "that we are frightful black lobsters. We rattle like them."

They slithered through a crack and came within sight of the flat rock above the pool.

There he was, sitting with his two tails crossed like legs, looking deserted and lonely in the streaming landscape. Seen close to he had dark blue eyes and hair like finest white crisp seaweed.

When he saw the two sou'westered heads peering

above a ledge, he shot like a frog into the pool and vanished from sight.

The boys let out a long Oh!, wild with joy that he was here, desolated that he had vanished. They scrambled recklessly and hung over the pool.

"He must come up to breathe," said Toby.

They waited, holding their own breath as long as they could in order to measure time. It was three of their longest before—either to breathe or from irresistible curiosity—the top of a seaweedy head, two very bright eyes and a nose came up in the far corner under some brown seaweed. The nose took a deep breath and sank under water, leaving only the eyes and hair showing, almost invisible in the dark hiding place. He watched the boys fixedly.

"If we took our clothes off," said Toby, "we should look more like him, and perhaps he'd like us."

"We haven't got tails," said Jo.

" 'Course we haven't. Wrap your clothes in your coat. It won't matter our being wet when we are bare."

The triton's eyes watched while clothes came off, and he even raised himself out of the water as this interesting operation went on.

"He thinks we are coming out of our shells like crabs," said Toby.

"I'm going to dress in seaweed. It will look more like a sea-person." Jo had a piece of string and was knotting sprays of loose seaweed on to it. He tied it on like an apron. Toby did the same with variations. He had a tail.

The little triton was hanging on to the edge of the pool

to see better. Finally two acceptable sea-boys drew near, holding out offerings, a spiral shell and a necklace.

As they lowered themselves into the water the triton submerged, but came up again somewhere else, and presently, advancing slowly and retreating hurriedly like a puppy being coaxed by strangers, he grew bolder. Jo's necklace was snatched first. At a little distance it was fingered, clicked to make its bead music, sucked, and finally put on.

Toby's arm was aching with holding out the spiral shell when at last it was taken, and with a frisk of his two tails the triton disappeared. He surfaced again in a moment and sat on a rock to look at his treasure. He emptied the water out of it, balanced it by its point, twirling it on the end of his first finger, put it to his ear and listened to it with deep attention. He gave Toby a quick bewildering grin. Then holding the shell in both hands he put the wide end to his lips as if he were playing the flute, and blew. An eerie sound of great sweetness came out, not unlike a curlew's call but with a peculiar hollow shell quality that was unmistakable.

The boys sprang towards him as though it were a summons that must be obeyed, and a reckless game began. The triton was always too quick for them and could hide under the clouded water longer. He would seize them suddenly by the ankles and upset them, to surface laughing himself, and if they caught him by one of his tails it was too slippery to hold. He was the wriggliest creature imaginable.

The rock pool was not big enough for such rough-and-tumble, though underwater knocks seldom make bruises. Before long the boys escaped on to the rocks, where the triton followed them, wriggling up and down faster than they could scramble, and nibbling the backs of their knees. Their legs were, of course, funny and strange. He had no rules against biting and looked innocently loving when they squealed.

"His tails are in the wrong place for wagging," said Jo as he bent to rub his leg with one hand and the triton's head with the other.

However, out on the sand it was left behind, only able to crawl. Once or twice it tried to get up on its tails as they did on their legs, but failed and was left far behind high and dry, making odd little protests that might have been seal talk. Toby came back and took it on his shoulders, where it locked itself, its muscular tails gripping him under the arms and twisting together behind. Toby ran for the sea, where Jo was waiting, and they flopped in together just before a playful wave heaved up and poured itself on to them, breaking them apart.

The triton lost his shell trumpet, and they all searched for it anxiously in the foam till the sea brought it back to its owner's hand. After that he never let it go.

The three played together entirely forgetful of time. With such a companion the sea itself ceased to be a stranger. The boys soon learned not to mind being under water. They quickly got the knack of having enough breath in their lungs at the right moment, of diving through the crest of a wave instead of being pounded by the fall, of treading water between waves as the triton did, and of riding back on them in the rough warming foam. They had been proud of the little swimming they could do before, and greatly in awe of the roaring sea, but today the waves, though rearing imposingly, had no real thrust behind them and were only turning over because they had met the shore, merely spilling their weight instead of using it as a battering-ram. Without thinking of it the boys became confident swimmers. Sometimes they held the triton's shoulders and were carried out of their depth and dived with him through the oncoming sea. Then when they needed a rest from swallowing the salt splash which got into their mouths when they tried to shout or were surprised laughing, they came on shore and gave the triton a turn on land, where they were the adepts. The rain which fell unnoticed all the time was like a soft water shower after the brine.

Jo tried to teach the triton to turn cartwheels. But for this he would have had to put down his precious shell, which he would not do. Toby solved the difficulty. The cowrie necklace was on a string of which the knotted ends had not been trimmed off. Toby had neat fingers, and though the triton would not let go of his trumpet nor part with his necklace, nor sit still, he managed to tie the two ends very tightly round the smallest spiral ridge at the point of the shell, and there was the wreathéd horn conveniently slung and loose enough to use. The triton was delighted and astonished.

"That was a very good idea," said Jo. "He doesn't need to cut his teeth. He's got them all. He seems to have hatched out very complete."

"So do ducklings," said Toby. "They swim right away. Perhaps all water things do."

Now that his hands were free the triton tried to copy Jo's cartwheels, but it was not until he was back in the sea that he could do it. There, in the line of shallow water between two long waves, he cartwheeled as expertly as a star-fish might. A ray of sunlight finding its way through a rift in the clouds lit him up momentarily as he sparkled along in a circle of spray. The oncoming wave caught his rosy tails in mid-air and he disappeared. Like a clown doing Hoop la! after a turn, he popped up behind the wave and blew his conch as applause for himself.

At this, there was an answering whoop from the far side of the cove, where now a seal's head was seen bobbing in the waves. She barked again on a higher note. Without a farewell look at Toby and Jo the triton shot away like a trout. They watched for any sign of him, but saw no more, and even the seal vanished.

At last far away, they saw the seal float out of a wave on to a rock, followed by an active sea-cupid and two sluggish silver-grey pups. The boys waved and shouted, and believed they heard a distant answering horn.

The cove was empty again, but now all was changed. The sea no longer looked to them cold and fish-coloured, but opaque with the warmer colour of tumbled sand, and it made the boulders look like seals as it swilled its brown glaze over them. Its sound came suddenly to their ears as if they had not been hearing it all the time. It rolled its living music over the beach again and again in light joyful crashes and seemed to promise an everlasting return.

The boys had a feeling of liberation and power. They were buoyant, turning homeward with songs and flags of seaweed, exhilarated and ravenous.

They shouted as they waded through the tunnel, and it made their voices hollow, elongated and multiple. It was

rougher going than they had had before. Sometimes the sea pushed them from behind, sometimes rushed at them from in the front, or came round both sides of the central pillar and caught them in its arms. When a swell higher than they expected made them bounce upwards and turned their singing to a squawk, the cave walls gave it back as a kind of sea-laughter mixed with the dripping waterfalls of spent waves. The boys felt it had become their tunnel, the gateway to their secret place, with the sea as guardian dragon to keep other people out, but not them.

Outside the tunnel their father was standing up to his knees in the foamy wash, under the pouring rain, trying to roll his trousers higher up his thighs to wade through, looking very grim. Their mother was climbing the headland over the tunnel to look at the cove on the other side. Their faces changed when they saw two elated sea-boys come out, dressed in seaweed skirts and showing all their teeth, partly because their smiles were so wide and partly because their teeth were chattering after so long a bathe.

Their mother came running and springing down to the edge of the water to meet them.

"Oh boys!" she said, thinking they looked confident and beautiful and splendid, "you are too provoking. It's hateful of you to frighten me so often."

"They're all right, as it happens," said their father, deciding not to be angry when he saw their look of happy success.

"We were perfectly sensible," said Toby. "We understand the tunnel."

"Where are your clothes?"

The boys' faces fell. Their sins rose up before them.

"We forgot them," said Toby. "We left them on the rocks. I think they must be washed away by now."

The thought amused Jo, who imagined their oilskins swimming hopelessly shoreward with weak empty arms. But he knew that wouldn't do. "We didn't seem to need them," he added.

"You are a pair of idiots," said their father. "Your mother is right. You ought never to be left alone. Now you have no mackintoshes, and we can't take you to the aircraft carrier dressed in seaweed."

"I like seaweed," said Jo unabashed. "I expect they'll be washed up tomorrow. The sea does put things back where it found them."

"Yes, under a ton of sand."

Jo found this funny too. "All right," he said. "Take us home and make us into decent English schoolboys."

"Then we can have some cocoa," said Toby.

After so much rain, the next morning was glorious, sunny and windy.

Having once played with a triton in the waves of a secret sea, the boys felt they could not live till it happened again. The desire ran through their veins, making them so restless they could not eat or settle to anything. All through breakfast they gazed through the window, interrupting their parents' conversation with sighs of, "Can't we go out yet?" "Why can't we go out now?"

"We will all go together and look for your oilskins. I suppose you know where you left them? It will be interesting to see how far they have travelled."

"Suppose they're in France?"

"Or wrapped round the screw of a boat?"

"Torn into ribbons like seaweed and hung over a rock so we will never see them?"

"Let us all sing rain coats' knell. I'll begin it. Ding Dong Bell," sang Jo.

"This is where we left them, by our rock pool."

"But that was at low tide. We must go up to the high tide mark."

Just below the line of driftwood and sea-wrack that marked high water, there was a bank of sand on which Jo's keen eyes spotted a button.

"Here's a button from one. Hi! It's sewn on to the sand!"

Much scratching and pulling uncovered one corner and then a whole oilskin coat deep in the firm grip of sand, sleeves full, pockets full, heavy and discoloured, and looking years older. It was Toby's.

"Rinse it in the rock pool. It will do, I think."

Jo had already slipped away from the others and was in the pool.

"Who's been trying on my coat?" he shouted as he fished it up. "Here's my hat too. I think somebody's been playing lobsters. I've got a starfish in my pocket!"

Toby rushed to look. "Let me see."

"Do you think it is a present?"

"It's alive. It's pretty."

"Put it in a pool. This one, with clear water."

The starfish's five arms, elegantly swaying, paddled it into hiding.

The parents were disciplinarian.

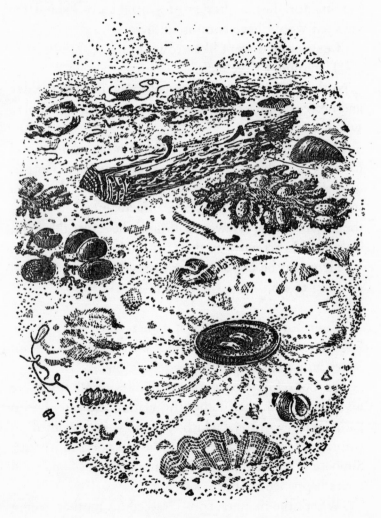

"Hang your coats over the rock to dry and help us to find the rest of your clothes."

The boys scrambled about looking in all the deepest and most difficult places, but it was not clothes they were looking for. Just a glimpse of a bright eye behind the seaweed would have comforted them.

"I expect he doesn't like grown-ups."

"They might have gaffs."

Nothing else was found, except much later in the day and nearer home a screwed-up green bag full of pebbles, which was Jo's shirt.

The search was called off, the day being much too good to waste in looking for what were only old shore clothes. The sky and the water were sapphire blue, the foam snow-white and sparkling, while the diamond flashes on the surface of the sea were so bright they hurt the sight. Toby and Jo screwed up their eyes to look.

"He might be bobbing about anywhere in it. It is too dazzling to see."

"Time for a bathe." Their father was calling them. "We are going back to the other side. Come on. I want to see how your swimming is getting on."

The boys followed perforce. Bathes at all times are joyful, and with their father stimulating and rare, but to bathe with a triton, which yesterday had seemed so natural, was now clearly seen to be too good to be true. Suppose it only happened once in a lifetime? Suppose it never happened again?

"What's the matter, Toby?" asked his mother, seeing

him standing transfixed with one arm still in the sleeve of his shirt. "You look like the knight alone and palely loitering."

"Nothing. Are you coming in?"

It's impossible to resist the invitation of the sea as it spreads a curtsey in a semi-circle of blue silk towards you, frilled with babbling foam that nibbles at your feet in the sand. Impossible to forget the first taste of blown salt on your lips as a translucent hollow wave as wide as the cove rises up before you, and, beginning at the far end, turns over its shrilling waterfall mane in one continuous movement all along the line till it breaks over your shoulders where you stand, and completes its perfect curl beyond, and now behind you. Once you are in it, the sea will never stop its challenge, pummelling with surf, jostling with crossed waves, tackling with the full weight of its spring, blinding with its wet white hair, pulling your legs from under you. It is, thought Toby, standing up breathless to await the next wave, the very stuff tritons are made of, and itself a measureless living thing.

His father was coming out of the sea with a triumphant Jo beside him. "Your turn, Toby. Come and show what you can do. I'm going to swim straight out to sea, and you come with me as long as you can possibly manage, then you can hold on to my shoulders and I'll bring you back."

Toby and Jo looked at each other, and Toby grinned.

When the bathe was over and they were all sitting in the hot sun, their mother said proudly, "They really can swim now, darling. To see them diving through waves you would think they were born in the sea."

"I know. We must have gone almost to the first of the Chain Rocks. It's marvellous how quickly they have learnt. I suppose it does come quickly once you have confidence."

"Some boys can swim right away the minute they're born," said Jo to his mother.

"So they say, my dear. 'Cast thy baby on the waters. Thou shalt find him after many days.' But I can't believe it. I didn't do it to you."

"I haven't tried in a really rough, angry sea," said Toby modestly. "But then even seals don't, not near the shore."

"I haven't tried a half-rough sea," said Jo. "Not a cross sea. I should be frightened at all that hissing, that is unless . . ." he hesitated and looked anxiously at Toby, "unless I had someone with me that the sea knew."

"You mean someone that knew the sea," said their father in a schoolmasterish voice.

"No, he doesn't," said Toby. "He means what he said."

The tide, which at the beginning of the holiday had been low in the morning, high by noon, and low again at bedtime so that most of the beaches were under water all day, had by now advanced till it was high morning and evening and lowest at midday. This meant a large expanse of sand most of the day, and as it was a fine Saturday many families would be coming down to enjoy it. The tunnel was passable between twelve and two, but before that only for people willing to wade a long way through deepening water.

Toby and Jo had been acutely aware, ever since they first woke up, of the hours of sea-privacy in that sealed-off cove. They knew every stone of it, and just where the waves would be swilling at any given moment, which pools would be deep and which shallow, and how the reflection of the rocks would re-form shakily in the smooth withdrawal between one probing influx and the next. Somewhere in that paradise of sun and flashing water, of shining boulders with the ghosts of spent waves hurrying down their curves into the sea, in the tang and the glitter and the eternal singing silence, there might be —if he had not left them forever—a companion that the sea had given them.

They had mooned about on the beach, watching the parties coming down laden with baskets and deckchairs, transistors and inflatable floating ducks, huge coloured balls, cricket stumps, bathing towels, dogs and babies, a complacent army of intolerable menace. Jo stood scowling and unresigned.

"It was not an ogre's soul in that egg," said Toby in a burst of passionate despair. "It was mine."

As soon as it was possible—and never had the tide seemed so slow in ebbing—the two of them were making their way towards the tunnel, trying to look as if they were going nowhere in particular, in order to give no one else the idea to follow. Their father and mother were bathing not far off, and had been so much relieved by the boys' new powers of swimming that they did not feel it necessary to watch them all the time, especially when the shore was so full of watchers.

This time when Toby and Jo reached the tunnel, the water was still so high that it was easier to swim than to walk. For the first time they swam through, submerging when the twisted waves looked rough and feeling very much creatures of the sea as they circled the half-way pillar and even dived to explore it underwater. At the farther end they shot through a transparent incoming wave and emerged into the great seclusion. They swam to shallower water and stood up to look round.

Perhaps what they really hoped was no more than to see the triton—for unless they saw him how could they be sure of him, how could they be pacified, how live until tomorrow—just to see him and warn him to be gone. They could not bear to have him glimpsed by the crowds. Toby imagined hordes rushing, shouting, pointing and jostling at the water's edge, throwing stones perhaps, sending in dogs, taking photographs.

"There's sure to be a B.B.C. commentator among all those," said Jo gloomily.

"Triton! Triton!" Toby called, cupping his hands round his mouth and trying to make a sound like a shell.

In the silence one wave after another ran in to the shore, with all their variations of water falling, running, dividing, re-uniting, swishing in its advance, whispering to a standstill, chattering in retreat. And then what could be the echo, or could be another wave doing the same thing further away. But no Triton.

The boys were heartbroken. They ran along the shore

calling, "Triton, Triton!" They went even beyond their rock pool and finally sat down on an island dome of rock covered entirely with thick long seaweed, parted in the middle as on a head.

"He's not anywhere," said Toby.

At that moment Jo gave a yell and jerked up his knee. Round the ankle was a hand that would not let go, and out from under the seaweed came the irresistible, ever-changing face, this time mock solemn. He rolled his eyes up to indicate the top of the cliffs, put a finger on his lips, and with a light kiss on Toby's calf such as a pup might give, or the sea itself, he withdrew. The boys felt among the seaweed curtains with their feet for a last touch of him, but he had vanished.

On the sky-line a party of people had appeared who were trying to find a way down the cliff, in which they were unsuccessful. But meanwhile others had found the tunnel and were riding through it knee deep on an inflated rubber horse, with wild shouts.

Toby and Jo returned with quiet assurance. Triton was real. He had not gone. They slipped through the tunnel, meeting only a large dog, walloping heavily through as part of a figure of eight expressing dogs' high spirits.

It was decided by the parents that Sunday was a dead loss as far as the beaches were concerned. They would be overrun. Buses were arriving every few minutes. The boys, though feeling that life was all waiting and suspense, one's heart always in one's throat, agreed that it was useless to stay. They went a long walk on the deserted uplands to visit prehistoric settlements. The sun blazed on slopes of withering grass as slippery as butter, and of the settlements not enough remained for the imagination to build on. Their father tried to make it interesting, but the boys were hot and tired. The only thing they could think of, and that with desperate longing, was the rush of sea-water over their bodies and the music of the sea in their ears. The cove was present in their minds in every detail for each of their five senses, clearer far than those bright close-ups in the field-glasses, and yet intolerably divided from them.

"I wish I could bathe," was all that Jo could say to relieve his too great desire.

"I believe the children are two changeling dolphins," said their mother.

"Then if we are changelings, where would your real children be?"

"I expect they are shrimpy sea-boys somewhere," she answered, laughing.

"Two?" asked Jo, astonished.

"Why not? One would be lonely."

The next morning when the boys were down on the beach collecting the bottles and tins and paper that yesterday's crowd had stuffed into all the nicest corners, wherever anybody would specially want to sit, their father came down to look for them.

"Good for you!" he said. "I'll help. When we have done this I want you to come up on the cliff. There are two young seals in your special cove, lying just above the tide mark."

This put the boys into top gear, and they were soon outstripping their father up the cliff path. They wanted to get there before him in the hope of a glimpse of the triton there too, but they saw only the great width of the sea with foam like marbling spread over it, and the narrow strip of rocks at the foot of the cliff, where the two seals were lying.

Seeing them on the land, the boys marvelled at the strange shape and bearing of these creatures. The two half-grown youngsters below them were speckled like young robins, with the faces of amiable teddy bears. Their bodies tapered away from powerful shoulders ending most oddly with a bear's tail and webbed feet pointing backward like a duck's when it swims. But most of all they were dog-like. One surprisingly was wearing a collar of some sort.

"Sea dogs," Jo said.

"No. That means sailors."

"Dog fish."

"That's something else."

"So is sealyham. And hams is just what these haven't got."

"Sea dachshunds then."

"Sea sausage dogs."

Both boys were thinking it was right and proper that a sea-boy should have a sea-dog, and these fabulous creatures were just right.

The seals lay across the rock as quietly as dogs on their own doorstep. They looked about the same size as Jo, but much fatter. They were not asleep. One of them looked up toward the voices on the cliff top, but appeared un-disturbed.

"If they stay here till the tide goes down, Daddy, could we go near them? Would they let us touch them?"

"I don't think young ones are fierce, but they may be shy. You can try."

The sun worked round till it shone full on the seals, who seemed to enjoy it, lying first on one side and then on the other, sighing in content.

At midday they slept, while the sea ebbed away from them.

Finally the boys and their father and mother came through the tunnel, and on seeing the seals still there Jo was not able to suppress a shout. The seals awoke, and went full tilt at a floundering legless gallop into the sea. Once in the shallows, however, they stopped and turned like curious calves to take stock of what had startled them.

"You stay behind," said Toby, barring the way for his parents with outspread arms and legs. "You'll frighten them, because you're grown-up. They perhaps won't mind things like us."

The boys approached the seals quietly. They felt no fear, and perhaps for that reason inspired none. To their coaxing noises the seals replied with sounds of curiosity. The boys lay down in the foam beside them.

All four bodies were rocked by the incoming waves. At first it was novelty enough to be sharing the sea with seals, floating with one's face so near to their large eyes that showed the whites as humans' and horses' do. The green collar was seen to be the remains of a fishing net.

By and by when they were all stranded together by the retreat of a wave, one of the seals rolled on to its side and lifted its flipper arm as a soppy dog does when it wishes to be scratched. Toby obliged, and Jo laughed when the flipper clearly signed go on much longer. And so acquaintanceship was begun, and soon they were playing catch in deeper water, the seals enjoying their superiority, though the boys had one advantage—they could seize and hold a struggling back flipper.

Presently they were all lying puffing in the swill again. Then Jo said—"Let's ride them." Toby ran to his heap of clothes on the beach and came back with a school tie that he knotted round the second seal's neck. They both straddled the seals' backs, that lying on the sand were as broad as ponies. They gripped the collars and dug their knees into the bulging fur. The seals, startled, immediately set off for the open water, bucking and tossing in the shallows so that no one could sit them, but the boys held on even if unseated. Once in the swim it was easier. The seals regained their slim shape and smooth action, and though the boys were frequently pushed off by waves, or slipped sideways when their agile mounts rolled or turned, they were thrillingly propelled through the water, and even found they had some control over the direction. When they were tossed, or let go and swam off, the seals came nosing round them with snuffling puppy talk.

It was too much for the parents to resist, and they came to join in. At this the seals made off at such a rate that their riders had to let go and swim back to shore. They came out laughing and satisfied. It had been a splendid romp. Their parents were surprised that the boys took both the adventure, and the sudden end to it, almost as a matter of course, but Toby and Jo were comparing it with the time spent with their secret companion. The seals had mild lumpy faces like puppies and the lovable furriness of all young animals, but their chief attraction was their being part of Triton's world, possibly even his messengers. Triton himself was of quite a different order, like laughter incarnate. His face was the face of the rapture-giving sea. They let the seals go and longed for Triton the more.

The days of the holidays were getting fewer and fewer, and now there were only three whole days left. It did not bear thinking about, but each day must be made to expand by as many packed moments as could be pressed into it. The boys wished only to stay in the same place, which promised inexhaustible marvels for them. Their parents wanted for themselves the interest of a different sea-scape to look at. Also they mistakenly thought the boys would learn more by seeing more places.

Willy-nilly Toby and Jo were taken away, heavy-hearted. It was two days since they had even glimpsed the triton, and now a whole day was to be thrown away.

"There's never time to live the things that are really important," said Toby sadly. Such experience surprised his parents.

It was another perfect day of kingfisher-blue sea and speedwell-blue sky, with a fresh little breeze coming in puffs to cool them off. And this was to be wasted as if it did not matter. As if it would come again. Sometimes things never came again. Toby kicked his heels on the floor of the car in a language of fury that his parents recognized and frowned at. Jo offered him a stick-jaw caramel.

"Be angry on this," he advised sympathetically.

They did not come back till nearly bed-time. The inner cove was cut off, but the boys ran up the cliff path on to the headland to see if the seals were on the beach.

They were not at first visible. The enormous vermilion sun was dropping toward the sea, its reflected glow making a blazing path across the water to the very beach, where the last ripple was spangled with garnets. Otherwise the sea was periwinkle purple, spilling and whispering, and sidling with an easy going prattle of foam round the steeper rocks.

When the sun had sunk into the haze of the horizon, its dazzle was dimmed to crimson, and then the boys were able to see two seals' heads bobbing far out in the line of its light. Flocks of seagulls flew by, coming from inland but all making for the island, where they dropped to earth without any preliminary circling, lifting their wings high, as though in such a crowd there was not room to put them down, and making a raucous screaming until the sun disappeared below the horizon. Then all was quiet, except for that murmurous half-telling, half-withholding of tremendous secrets that the sea would keep up all night. Each little wave seemed to say, "I'll tell you——" and then pull back with a smothered, "Oh!" to be followed by another wave saying, "Then I will say——" but whatever it was remained unsaid and unsayable.

The boys went homewards full of the feeling that the sky, the sea and the land were more than they seemed to be, and perhaps even quite different. They wound their way down among the rocks like prehistoric boys homing before the approach of the great goddess Night. Already the evening star was visible.

The night that was approaching held nothing of either darkness or coolness. The sun had hardly removed its rosy afterglow in the west before the moon-dawn had begun in the east. Soon the moon itself, full and brooding, was transforming everything as powerfully as any enchantress.

The boys' parents were going to a party at a friend's house an hour's drive away. The boys were seen into bed and told that the landlady, Mrs. Ship, would be there if they wanted anything, but they were not to stay awake for their return, because it might not be till early morning.

Toby and Jo heard the car go away, up the near hill, change up, change down, up the far hill, fainter, and gone.

Their window was wide open in the hope of air, but the earth was smothered in warmth and could not cool off. They lay in the big bed, too hot for any bedclothes, with the rising moon looking in through the window.

Its light fell across their faces, and could be felt, as sun-light can. This feel of the moonlight was not in the nature of hot or cold, but something indescribable.

"It is supposed to do something to people and dogs," said Toby.

"What sort of things?"

"It makes them wander and do things."

"Do you feel like wandering?"

"I don't know. It's queer."

"I feel all prickly. I'll never go to sleep."

They tossed and turned in the flood of magic light, and when they sat up they saw each other's faces ghostly and beautiful.

"Shall we draw the curtains to shut it out?"

"No. We wouldn't hear the sea."

"Shall we get out and look?"

Their bedroom was on the ground floor, but the cot-tage stood on a low bluff just above the home beach, giving a wide view of the sea.

Toby and Jo gasped as they looked out. The curving sky, so much bigger than it looks by day, was distant with faint stars that seemed to hang in their places, but the glorious moon was riding up. It dominated every-thing, even the vast sea that spread under it a creamy silver-blue floor bigger than anyone could think. Across this came now the white pathway of the moon, and the ripples broke in sparklets.

The familiar promontories and rocks looked strange, with bleached silver faces and deep black chasms. The solitary rocks jutting out of sea and sand were like watchers or crouching animals, and there were more shadowy lurking places, if you found yourself imagining lurking things. Yet the whole impression was shockingly beautiful. Only the moon was real, all the rest was dream and faerie.

Toby and Jo leant out in the tepid air. There was nothing to hear but the sea, and of that they heard more the more they listened. They could recognize the sound of waves in special places, over this rock or that, into hollows and through cracks, or mixing with the babble of the stream. The tide, they thought, must be nearly full.

"I feel a sort of pulling," said Jo hopefully.

Toby gave a deep sigh. "I wish we could see Triton cove from here."

Somewhere outside there was a sound that turned both boys into unbreathing statues.

"Could it have been?" said Jo, looking into Toby's face and seeing it as something he had never seen before, with an unearthly eagerness in it.

It came again—the unforgettable, unmistakable Triton's horn, from somewhere in Home Cove.

Both boys were out of the window and padding down the sandy track in their pyjamas before they even thought. Mrs. Ship's window was at the back of the cottage and she did not see them go. They went slowly like sleepwalkers in the strange light in which they could both see and not see, as all distances were different and their bare feet had to feel for the uneven ground whose dips were hard to judge.

They came to the edge of the sea and stood silhouetted

against the moon-path, their shadows black as dogs behind them.

The triton's call came again.

Between the shore and the island there was a series of
low rock islands fairly evenly spaced, all lying in the
moon-path, though the island itself was just outside it.
The summons seemed to come from the nearest of these
stepping-stones, on whose outline there was an added
shape.

Toby and Jo stripped off their pyjamas and threw
them on the shore. The water felt warmer than it does by
day. There was no shock of cold on entering, but a great
thrill at the touch of gilded glinting water.

They swam side by side like dogs to a whistling master.
It was perhaps already as far as they had been with their
father, but they swam not so much with confidence as
because they had not yet had any thought except that
they were coming. In this shining pathway there was
neither time nor distance, nor any feeling that this was as
far as they dared go, for it went to the moon, and that is
outside calculation.

They had learnt by now that it is not necessary to
swim frantically to keep afloat. The least movement will
do. The seals had taught them the art of being leisurely in
water, of rolling over in it at their ease. They passed
through shoals of small fish, whose tiny tail flicks tickled
their bodies. It felt like swimming in sodawater. If the
summons had not been imperative, they would have
been tempted to float on their backs and look at the
moon and stars, and kick up sprays of moonlit water, and

dream better than in their beds. But they must join Triton first.

It is difficult when swimming to see far ahead until you are quite clear of the incoming waves however gentle, but from time to time they heaved up to look at the rock that they were making for.

Presently they saw Triton sitting on it. His trumpet glinted in the moonlight. He had grown since they last saw him and looked about him with young authority. The moon shone on his face so that it looked as if it were made out of mother-of-pearl.

He pulled the boys up on to the ledge beside him and looked from one to the other smiling. They saw that he was wearing a wide gold band on his upper arm. From what drowned wreck or undersea cavern had he taken that? It made his necklace and horn look royal.

Jo made him a bow. Sitting out there on a rock in the moonpath you could do whatever you felt like. Toby did the same.

The triton laughed out loud and shot into the water. The boys still needed a moment to rest. They sat there looking about them—back to the land where no light showed from their cottage, up at the white hypnotizing circle of the moon, and higher up still whence falling stars were flying in long curves toward the west. Then they heard the triton's horn from the next rock. He blew it twice urgently, and they followed.

At the third rock they realized that they were going to the island. It was now nearer to them than the shore. As the moon rose higher, her path over the sea widened and dispersed, till it formed a circle like a reflection of the moon magnified a million times and frittered into softness, and in this the island reared up with its dark side toward them.

The tide was full and lazy. It heaved like the deck of a ship, the wash sliding along the sheer side of the island with nothing that could be called a wave. These could be seen far behind in even lines of shining play outlining the cove.

Triton's white hair shone like moon-foam too, and his bright eyes and white shell regalia showed up in the shadow cast by the island cliff when they finally reached it. His will-o'-the-wisp presence guided them round its base till they reached the seaward side, where the arches in full moonlight stood up desolate and awe-inspiring. Further out still was the broken rock barrier on which even a waveless sea was torn and continually remade itself.

The cliff in which the mouths of the caves opened, that had looked so dark against the midday sky, was now gleaming like old silver, and into the central cave flowed a bright tongue of water, flecking the sides with its own reflected pattern. Into this the boys, unable to believe it was really happening, swam after their leader, and at the entrance a heave of the sea took them and bore them in.

The whole interior of the cave was rounded and polished by the sea. Not a particle remained in it that could be wrenched off or carried away. To the hands and feet it felt like the inside of a shell, and a milky twilight of sea-shine half-lit it almost to its length. It seemed to stop short after about fifteen yards, and the faint light relaid in flickers from the lapping water showed the end of it as darkly gleaming rock.

There were ledges of stone where the sides of the cave had been scooped away by the sea and on these the boys sat to rest and to accustom their eyes to the curious non-darkness. Triton was in great excitement, whisking and flashing about, provoking and caressing the boys as rough young things do, who only don't hurt because they don't want to. At last he straddled a jutting rock and blew his conch so that the cave re-echoed with a haunting sound as of many sea-creatures calling.

Something soft brushed by Jo's leg. A seal. As his eyes learnt to interpret the movements of less or more dark and light in the cave, he saw the humped backs of seals, like overturned canoes, swim in from the sea. Toby saw them too. They came in, dark against the moonlight, and they vanished. The boys tried to follow them with their eyes, and after a while became aware that at the end of the cave, where they would have expected the water to be darkest, it was in fact clearest, as if lit up dimly from below. And now they could see the seals pass like ghosts down into it and fade away. This must be the underwater tunnel.

"It looks," murmured Jo, daring for the first time to speak in this other-world place, "like looking through an aquarium. Water is like glass."

"There must be light at the other end, more than here."

"I wonder how far away it could be."

But now the triton was impatient, pulling them and

then diving down toward the drowned light. They clung to their ledge and watched the shadowy flick of his two tails vanish. In a short time they saw him returning and he surfaced shaking diamonds from his hair. Had he turned to see if they were following, or had he been there and back to show them it was not far? While they hesitated, as well they might, Triton lifted himself up half out of the water where a ray of outer moonlight struck in and showed his face like a young Neptune with a frown of impatience.

This was more than Toby could bear. He stretched out his arm, which was seized round the wrist, and in a moment both he and Triton had vanished into the glimmering depth.

Jo was left alone. His heart pounded as he held his breath in sympathy with Toby till he was nearly bursting. Would that be long enough? He was seeing stars. Could Toby do it longer than he could? It hurt. He gasped desperately and found himself almost eating the wonderful comforting air. And Triton was there again, commanding.

"If he can do there and back, I can do there," was Jo's last thought as he took as much breath as he could and plunged. Down, down, trailed by Triton's strong pull. It is easy to hold your breath if you don't swim, he thought. If it doesn't go on too long. His head began to buzz, he felt the upward turn, he could hold out if he must, he must, he must—and he was there, swimming in a ruined sea palace, lit by a broad shaft of moonlight through an upper opening like a clerestory window.

His ears, still singing from holding his breath so long, for a moment did not bring to him the utterly unexpected noise that filled the place, murmuring, hooting, squealing and singing such as might be heard at a water fairy's party, and so echoing overall that he did not hear

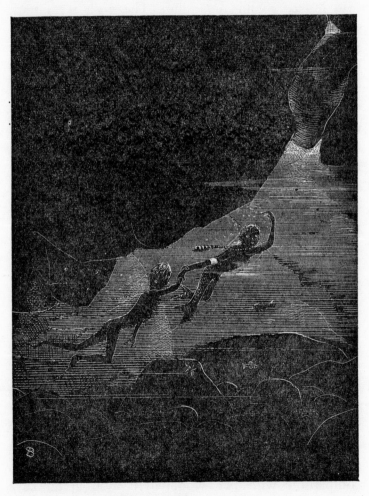

Toby calling to him. He saw him however, sitting laughing on the rocks with two seals beside him, one wearing a green collar and one a school tie. Jo joined him, and patted his seal, glad to have another friend after his ordeal. The seal wriggled in acknowledgement.

Jo looked round about him. The walls were stark sheets of rock, widely cracked, in places gaping or tilted. Sloping monolithic buttresses propped them where they leaned inward too much, and also supported what was left of the roof. Exaggerated moon-shadows fell like black velvet curtains over angles and recesses, and striped the silvered floor. It was a savage and spacious fortress against the sea. Tumbled stones round the sides sloped to the water, and on these many seals were hauled up, their speckled breasts hard to distinguish from the dappled shadows. It was they, and others out of sight, who were making all the noise. Nearby was a mother, grunting softly to her two pups, perhaps the very one who had been Triton's foster mother. She barked over their heads at other seals who came too near. Half-grown youngsters hooted and squealed as they played. Others, perhaps the oldest, were singing, a wild, sad, up and down song of the most ancient ocean. Their powerful throats could produce soft notes of great carrying power. Every now and then there was a deep note like a fog horn. Or were they perhaps singing to the moon, the magnet of tides? Through the upper opening she could be seen moving through absolute silence, high and splendid with stars behind her, dazzling beyond comparison with her wobbly reflection in the cave pool, where there were also stars, chased by the ripples of surfacing seals.

Where was Triton all this time? Had he brought them here to see this wonder, and then left them? Toby and Jo searched the darker places anxiously, and saw him at last, sitting astride a big bull seal on a raised place at the far end. It was the bull who made the fog-horn sounds. And now Triton sang too—a high song that excited the seals so that all their chins went up in a wailing assent at every verse end.

This varied and repetitive din after a time came to seem natural, and even possible not to hear, like the sea itself. But presently a new sound crept in, that was felt rather than heard, a faint purposeful throbbing, but whether it was heard through the roof or transmitted, muted, through the underwater passage, the boys could not tell. The whole seal gathering reacted to it with yelps, swaying their long necks. In the shadows they looked like huge snakes coming out of their holes.

They were greatly excited and clearly anxious to go. But Triton was their leader and he was the first to leave. He shot past the boys and dived into the exit. He blew his horn down there and bubbles came up, giving out a parody of its sound. The old bull seal went next, and all in their order rapidly after him, so that the mouth of the tunnel danced with bubbles and eddies. Toby and Jo saw themselves soon to be left behind in this eerie place where no one could ever find them, and they thought perhaps the seals were leaving in terror of something of which they had no notion. The throbbing was like their racing hearts. When their two seals moved to wallop down, they desperately hung on to their collars as the only sure way to get out.

Under water the throbbing was louder, till it was lost in the noise in their ears and the pain in their chests, but at last the seals surfaced at the other side. They travelled so fast that the boys simply held on, their legs flowing out behind them. Because of the pull on their necks the seals swam on the surface or with very slight undulating dives, and the boys were able to breathe.

They found themselves travelling effortlessly across a wide opal sea that danced past their faces with a continuous glitter of sea-stars, under the infinite yet comforting sky, with its great creature the moon riding through it on air, as they were riding on water. It was all so strange and dreamlike that they took it as it came, almost without surprise, as one takes the impossible in dreams. They did not ask themselves—what shall we do if the seals make for the open sea? The seals were making for Home Cove and even that now looked a very long way off. Ahead of them could be seen the lights of an inshore trawler, whose engine it must have been that drummed in the underwater passage, attracting the seals.

As they drew near they could see the crew getting ready to haul up the net, and then their seals dived in earnest and they had to let go and swim. Toby saw that Jo was there close at hand. The men on the trawler were shouting to each other and the skipper swearing in proper sea fashion, so that such poor shouts as swimmers can give were not heard. The boys, suddenly very tired, feel-

ing like people who have never learnt to swim, wh[ose]
legs go down, reached the boat as the trawl was bei[ng]
hauled up. The boat rode high and overhung them, an[d]
there was nothing they could catch hold of but a loop o[f]
rope. Clinging on to this, they saw the net emerge lop-
sidedly, with a seal-sized hole in the bottom through
which a shoal of fish poured past them into the sea, like
quicksilver into quicksilver.

A man with a lantern leant over the stern to free the
rope on which the boys were clinging.

"God Almighty! We've got two corpses in the net,"
he yelled. The clamour broke out again, faces peered
over, and when it was seen that the boys were alive and
hanging on with difficulty there was instant help and a
burst of outrageous jokes.

"Of all the beautiful catches! A pair of darned boys!"

"Won't the skipper be pleased!"

"Would you believe it!"

"Where are 'e from, my loves?"

"Out of the everywhere into here!" said Jo, nettled.

There was a shout of laughter.

"Naked as the day they was born too."

"We don't wear our clothes in the sea," Jo said with
dignity.

"He's a proper caution."

The skipper loomed up with a grim face.

"Get the lights on. Stand by with the lifebelt. Keep a
look out. Now, boys. You're all right. Are there any
more of 'e?"

"I thought I saw a third, a boy with white hair," said

battered toothless little old fellow whom nobody took much notice of.

"No," said Toby with chattering teeth. "There's only us. Jo and me."

"Maybe it was one of them," said the old man apologetically. "They's got whitish hair too. My eyes aren't what they was."

"Lend them sweaters, somebody," said the skipper. "Now, lads, where's your boat?"

"There's no boat," said Toby, feeling warmer in a thick fishy sweater, but reduced to a boy who was a nuisance and would have to give an account of himself.

"What the hell do you mean, no boat? I suppose you are swimming round the world to get a medal for enterprise? You've followed the Gulf-stream here from Cape Hatteras? Say something we can believe."

Toby could think of nothing to say that would be believed, but Jo, busily pulling up the elephant trunk sleeves of his sweater which reached the ground, as soon as he could find his hands said with a candid smile:

"We were having a midnight bathe by ourselves and we got sort of carried away. Of course we know we shouldn't have."

"Where are 'e from then?"

"Home Cove."

"And you got carried out from Home Cove with the tide at full?"

One of the crew pushed forward with two mugs of cocoa. It was their friend the lobster man.

"Good life! What have us here? You two fished up in the trawl! Yes, Skipper, I know them. They're staying with my aunt, Ada Ship, in the Cove."

Jo looked at the lobster man, who seemed in these circumstances a very old friend.

"We've seen the seals," he said, confidentially. Toby frowned at him, but at the word seals wrath broke out again on the ship.

"Don't talk to me about seals," said the skipper. "Look at that something great hole in the net. A hundred pounds ran out at that hole and that's that for tonight. Well, we've got to get these perishing little blighters home. If their tale's true I suppose they will be missed, and whether it's true or not, if the police were called in we don't know what we'd be in for. We might even be accused of kidnapping the naked mother's darlings. At the best it would mean a day in the police station answering questions instead of being in bed."

"But you rescued us!" said Toby indignantly.

"The question is, how did you come to be there to be rescued? I've been trawling these waters since I was fifteen, and never before met two naked babies swimming about on their own in the bay."

The boys were offended.

"We can swim," said Jo.

"You bet you can swim. You needed to. What the hell are we to do with them, Sam? All the police in the country will be out looking before we get into port. Home Cove looks quiet enough yet. No lights showing. I'll have to cruise around here awhile yet just in case

83

there are any others to be picked up, or the boat loose. Whose boat would they have, Sam?"

"Mine I suppose; it's the only one beached there."

"We didn't have a boat," Toby repeated.

"I saw your father and mother going off by car," said Sam. "Were you on your own?"

"Mrs. Ship is looking after us," said Jo.

"Then Mrs. Ship is in for a packet of trouble when this comes out," said the skipper.

"There's someone putting out from the Cove now, Skipper. That's my engine. It'll be my brother Bob. He's maybe going out after pollock."

"Hail him as soon as you can."

The boat was hailed, and the occupant proved to be Bob. He drew in beside the trawler and the skipper and Sam explained the situation. As far as Bob knew, the boys had not been missed. He was hoping to go out after pollock, but would take the boys home.

"Look, Skipper," said Sam. "I don't want the old lady upset. She'd be a laughing stock, and she'd never get over having the police come round at her. Let Bob try to get them in the way they got out, without attracting attention, unless the place is buzzing by the time he gets there. And if the boys are with him the fuss will die down. He can say they were just off the shore. Get along now, you two. Get home and say nothing. We've all been up to mischief in our time."

"I don't like it," said the skipper. "It looks mighty fishy to me."

They were taken away in the little boat by Bob. The

84

trawler was turning her lights in a sweep over the untroubled water.

"There's nobody else," said Toby, and leaning against each other, the boys fell asleep.

When the boat was beached, Bob tried to shake them awake.

"Did you have any clothes? Mustn't leave anything lying about. And the lads will want their jerseys back."

"Pyjamas," said Toby on a yawn, his eyes still shut. With Bob's help these were found not far away, and with fumbling uncertain movements they put them on. If they had left the cottage feeling like sleep-walkers, it was as real ones that they returned. Toby sat half-way across the window-sill and remained there fast asleep. Bob lifted them both over and put them into bed.

As he was returning from the cottage he stumbled on a loose stone and clicked the gate louder than he should have done.

Immediately a window opened upstairs, and Mrs. Ship called out, "Who's there?"

"It's Bob, Auntie. Just shutting your gate as I went past. Going to the boat."

"All right, Bob; thank you. I thought it was my lodgers coming home. I'm in charge of the children till they do."

"Any trouble?"

"Not a bit. Not a sound all night. As good as angels. There's a car now coming over Camp Hill. That'll be their parents I guess."

"I'll be getting on then. Good night."

When their parents tiptoed in to the boys' bedroom, they were sleeping so soundly a bomb would not have wakened them. The moon had gone up and over on her course and no longer shone on their faces, but as their mother looked at them she sensed a difference. Perhaps it was the way they were lying, as if they had literally fallen into bed without a thought of arranging their limbs for sleep.

"If I only leave them for an evening," she said sadly, "they seem more grown-up when I come back. Don't they look different to you, darling?"

"I can imagine they do, if you say it. I feel years older myself since that party." And late in the morning, yawning in his bed, he groaned that he would have to get up, or the boys would be either bothering or vanishing.

"They are still asleep. I think we must have over-tired them yesterday. I don't think long car drives are good for them, and it was terribly hot. We won't go anywhere today."

"Thank goodness for that," he said, turning over to sleep again.

Most of the morning, which was the last but one, was over before the boys woke up. Jo opened his eyes, fresh from long, deep, dreams and looked about him. It was sunny and the window curtains were flapping in a lively breeze. Brisk waves were rollicking up the shore below, and there was a din of seagulls.

"Toby!" he said softly. "Do you remember last night?"

87

"Yes. I remember everything. But I don't remember getting back into bed."

"Let's get up and go and talk to Sam."

"The bed's full of sand. Better sweep it out."

"It looks more natural on the floor."

Their mother was sitting on the garden wall waiting when they appeared, dressed and brushed and thinking only of food.

"Can I have two eggs for breakfast?"

"I told Daddy you had grown up in the night, so I suppose you do need double. He's still in bed."

"If he grows too, we shall never catch up."

"What a future stretches before me! On my tombstone they will put, 'She was small, but the wife and mother of giants.' "

The family settled themselves against a shoulder of rock where they were out of the wind, which was fresher than they had thought.

"You wouldn't think it was the same sea," said Toby as they sat watching it, content to do nothing. He was thinking of the enchanted, lulling ocean that had borne him and Jo on its silver-gilt plain in concord with the moon. Today it was obstreperous with animal spirits let loose, churning up the sand and slapping the cliffs, not so much rough as excited.

The two boys were unusually quiet. For them, the sun and the air and the smooth stones to choose from, were enough.

"You are a moony pair," said their father. "Don't you want to do anything? I must say, I don't."

"Every day doesn't have to be special," said Toby wisely.

"Did you enjoy yesterday specially?"

Toby looked at his mother with startled query. Then he remembered there had been an excursion.

"Well, it was a different cove," he said casually. "Quite different." He returned to his sifting of stones, and having made a collection of flat ones, he began with a sharp edge to draw seals on them.

"I'll fill the shore with seals," he said.

Jo sat watching, or went to choose more stones. From time to time, as he came and went, he sang a few very strange and haunting notes, always the same. His mother listened to him.

"What are you singing, Jo? I have never heard it before."

"It's my seal song."

"Has it any words?"

"No. It's just a song."

"How does it go on?"

"I can't remember any more," he said with an unexpected shake in his voice.

Toby handed him a stone with a different picture on it. "You can keep that."

"It's very good," said Jo. "I like it. Flip! and he's gone."

"There's Sam. Let's go and talk to him."

"I'll come too," said their father. "I've got to pay him for the boat to Drift Cove."

Sam was opening up his souvenir shop.

"Good afternoon, sir." He gave the boys an exaggerated wink. "How are you all today?" He looked knowingly at Toby and Jo and made swimming movements with his hands. The boys were very uncomfortable.

"I suppose your time here is nearly up. You've had wonderful weather. We can't expect it to go on so late in the season. It's changing now. There'll be no more seas like yesterday's. You'd better take these two boys home before they get a taste of the real stuff. That would surprise them. We'll get it any time now."

"I'd like to see a real storm," said Toby. "How big are the waves then?"

"I couldn't say how high they are, but they look over the island at you."

"Would the island be under the sea?" asked Jo, thinking of the window opening high up on the cliff face.

"No, not that. But it's almost lost in spray."

"I hope there will be a storm tomorrow, a very big one."

"You shouldn't want that. You wouldn't if you knew."

As if in answer to these words, there came from far away the sound of the Triton's horn. The boys turned to gaze out to sea, and heard it repeated from another direction, and again from quite near, and then an eerie chord as three sounded together. The calls drew closer together, like birds assembling, till with a mingled whistling and fluting that tugged at the boys' hearts, they passed growing fainter and fainter, out to sea.

"What were those?" said their father after a surprised silence.

"I don't know, sir. I've never known what those can be. I never see the flight like you see sand pipers swirling along. Myself, I call them storm birds. I don't hear them often, but when I do, I know summer's over. They're going south."

"To the Mediterranean?" said Toby, profoundly moved.

Jo clutched Toby's shirt. "He's found the others," he whispered.

"So that's all right," said Toby slowly and sadly. "And we can go home after tomorrow. It won't matter."

All that day the wind blew as the tide worked itself up to the full and fell back again with threatening roars and grumbles. At tea-time, when they could have passed the tunnel, the boys had no wish to. That was finished now.

All night the wind buffeted the cottage, rattled the windows, shrieked through keyholes and sent gusts down the chimneys that shook the house. It helped to muffle the stormy racket of the night tide.

By morning a full gale was blowing. It was difficult to stand up against it, and not only did it give violent thrusts, far more alarming was the pull of its moments of vacuum. Sam warned the family not to go on the cliffs, where the wind could suck them off. They stood, or rather staggered, constantly thrown off balance, on the shore, hearing, between the howls of wind, the distant sea like continual express trains. The wind was full of sand and salt and skinned their faces and legs.

"You asked for it," shouted Sam. "It'll be a tide all right at noon. And worse tonight."

The white and angry sea seemed to leave out low tide impatiently and start its forward urge under pressure. It began to surge in with waves twice the usual size and force, so that when they hit the cliffs the rebound was almost equally strong and cut through the following crests. Inside the cove this happened from both sides, causing the central sea to buck and jostle, frustrated of its movement, and to seethe with anger. Sometimes the rebound from the cliff and a new wave met head-on in a smack that sent fountains of spray high above the headland. Already in this way the surf was "looking over the island". From distant caves came a steady Boom! Boom! as of quarrying. Now and again a particularly powerful wave would form itself with a long foaming head and muscle its way through the tumult with a tearing roar, throwing up stones ahead of it. The air re-echoed with toppling crashes, whip-cracks and the high rattle of shingle, over a continuous fiendish rumble.

By noon there was a new development. Out to sea appeared a series of high ridges like the roof tops of whole Cornish streets, one behind the other. They came from the horizon moving steadily in threes, marbled but forming no crests until they were well up the slope of the cove. There they suddenly rose to a towering height, a crest sprang up with terrifying instantaneous ease, and they broke with a roll of thunder and a drumming that shook the shore. The water pushed before these rollers swirled inland far beyond the normal reach, rolling boulders up the slope that clattered and bounced backward in the retreat.

Sam, sheltering with them all behind a breast-high rock, said that these ridges came from far out in the Atlantic, and were much to be feared. From time to time, without warning there had been big ones that had swept like tidal waves beyond the shore, up the valley. He had now shuttered his shack and was about to shutter-up Mrs. Ship's cottage, where already the spray was rattling on the windows like pebbles.

"Take my advice, sir," he said seriously. "Move up to the hotel for the night. There's plenty of room now the season's over. I have to be on lifeboat duty tonight. Any ships that haven't managed to keep out of this will be in trouble."

"Won't the lifeboat be, too?" asked Toby.

"Sure it will. A whole lot. There's no knowing what tonight will be like, sir. I wouldn't let Auntie stay here alone. The cottage even might be breached."

The boys were round-eyed.

Sam laughed, rather wryly. "These young gentlemen don't know nothing about the sea yet."

The family, sufficiently impressed by what they saw and heard, packed up and left, taking Mrs. Ship with them to drop her at Sam's house. The boys looked back out of the rear window as the car revved up the steep lane and rocked in the wind.

Across the heaving turbulence and flying foam enormous rollers were slowly moving in. The last thing Toby and Jo saw was a wild burst of spray entirely hiding the island.